PANTO BOY

The Dive Diaries Book Two

PANTO BOY

A Romantic Comedy With A Twist

DIVA DIARIES
BOOK 2

KERRIE NOOR

CONTENTS

PANTO BOY

Book Two Diva Diaries
By
Kerrie Noor

JUST A THOUGHT

Pantomime is the language of comedy…
So Deirdre was to find out.

GLOSSARY

Meat and Two Veg: A traditional British meal which has vegans running for their tofu.

Chippy: A fish-and-chip shop traditionally famous for battering anything, including Mars Bars and haggis.

Saga magazine: An informative magazine for the over-fifties spinning the yarn that getting older is "Fab."

Malarkey: A fun word to use instead of *drivel*, *rubbish*, or *piffle*, although *piffle* is a pretty good word too.

Bahoochie: A fun but unpronounceable word best left to the Scots to use—meaning the luscious cheeks of a backside.

Night Nurse: Nothing to do with nursing, but a cold remedy so strong that you can sleep though the crowing of a cock and three alarms.

The Two Ronnies: An all-male British comic duo who inspired many comedians to cross-dress despite looking like wrestlers.

Stanley Baxter: A Scottish comedian whose impressions of the queen had me cackling into my haggis.

Les Dawson: An English comedian who was known for his satirical piano playing and impressions of housewives with no teeth, large chests, and a penchant for gossip.

Jamie Oliver: If you don't know Jamie Oliver, you may as well shut the kitchen and call in a pizza.

1

VEGAN IS THE NEW BLACK

An audience is not the be-all and end-all.

*D*eirdre moved in with Agnes after her husband, a meat-and-two-veg man, had decided that he no longer wanted to be married to a woman whose idea of "meat and two veg" was a nut loaf with "green stuff."

Deirdre, a little relieved, rented a run-down shop next to Poundstretcher. She cleared the mouse droppings, painted a mandala, and started dabbling in herbs and anything organic. Deirdre's Vegan is the New Black shop was her dream, a fantasy that had kept her going for years.

"Vegetables are fun," she used to say to her husband, which usually had him choking on his sausages. He hated vegetables and would not consider eating one except when grated, camouflaged or stuffed into meat.

Vegan is the New Black was slow to pick up. In fact, Deirdre was so out of pocket she was forced to move into the back of the shop to save money. Vegetables and soya were sniffed at by most, and it was only when she splashed out on a window display of her new Goddess and Beyond creams that women began to show interest.

Along with her vegan food, Deirdre made creams and potions for stretch marks, wrinkles, and achy joints. And when women started asking for more, Deirdre, working harder, upped her production. Soon, she told herself, she'd be as busy as the chippy down the road; all she needed was a bit of luck and a marketing plan as cheap as a packet of crisps.

It was autumn when Agnes visited the Vegan is the New Black shop. She walked in stiff-lipped and headachy. She had spent the best part of a morning arguing with her partner about the whole "principal boy thing."

Agnes had an audition for the local panto and, as usual, was "going for" the principal boy. Agnes had a strut worth watching, and she knew it; every year she pulled out her leggings, extra-high boots, and a fetching hat to do just that: strut through her audition.

The principal boy was the be-all and end-all to her. Standing onstage singing "All the Nice Girls Love A Sailor" and the like was heaven to her, she loved camp, dressing up and applause. And now at the ripe old age of sixty-five she wanted one last bite of the cherry.

Her partner Lesley, however, had had enough. For years she protested; George's pantos filled her with dread. Every autumn she moaned to a blank face, deaf ears, and a parade of leggings, hats and hopeful "What do you think?" looks. Agnes fretted about her age, and over the years preparing for her audition had turned into a series of "do I look old in this?" moans that pushed Lesley's patience to the limits.

Once the panto season started, Lesley hardly saw Agnes, apart from times when Agnes, anxious about her age, demanded feedback about her latest costume. Appearing with a "gorgeous or what?" pose, Agnes would stand in front of the TV, usually at a crucial moment; the punch line of a joke, the winner of *Strictly Come Dancing* or, worse of all, *Gardener's Question Time*.

Lesley lived for the day that Agnes would hang up her hat and join her on the couch. When they could plan the garden, bet on who wins *Strictly Come Dancing*, or laugh at a punchline together.

In fact, she was so desperate she organised a surprise sixty-some-thing, birthday-come-retirement party. Lesley had high hopes that Agnes would take the hint and give up.

The panto players presented Agnes with a "have a great retire-ment" shield along with a year's subscription for *Saga* magazine. Lesley even took Agnes on a retirement cruise and was stunned into silence when Agnes waltzed into the kitchen sporting velvet leggings, leather boots, and a "ta-da" pose.

Lesley looked up from her bacon and exploded.

"I thought we agreed that you were to stop all this malarkey."

"Malarkey? Panto is hardly malarkey," said Agnes.

"But the cruise, the panto shield, the *Saga* magazine . . ."

Agnes sighed. "I need this."

"This?"

"Treading the boards, the standing ovations."

"No one does standing ovations in Lochgilphead."

Agnes threw her a look.

"Don't know why you frigging bother," muttered Lesley.

Agnes pouted.

"No one gives a monkey about that knob George and his productions."

"I do."

"That man's pantos have taken boredom to a whole new level. And as for that bubbling fool Derek, watching him play the dame is as painful as stepping on an upright plug."

"But I'm not . . . painful to watch," said Agnes.

"It's just a wee panto, in a wee church hall for old folks; even the schoolkids are dragged along under the promise of a free McDonald's."

"That's a total exaggeration," said Agnes, "there's no McDonald's for miles."

"Just once I would like a normal winter: you, me, and *Strictly Come Dancing* on the telly."

Agnes slumped. "I hate *Strictly*."

"Why don't you take up gardening with me?"

Agnes pulled a face.

"Walking then?"

"Walking? I am a dancer, a master of the high kick."

Lesley tutted.

"Just one last dance, that's all I want."

Lesley, scraping butter onto her toast with venom, scowled.

"Is that too much to ask?" said Agnes.

Lesley muttered a "flabby around the chops" insult, squeezed her bacon into a sandwich, and headed into the garden.

Agnes, with a sigh, pulled a few faces in the mirror. Was her jaw flabby? Was she too old? She twisted to see her bum, held in her stomach, and then pulled a red-carpet pose. Maybe a better bra, a tan?

Then she remembered Deirdre's Goddess and Beyond shop display. The chemist who had smooth, tanned skin had not stopped talking about it, and she should have retired years ago . . .

2

THE STORE ROOM

When it comes to store rooms, size matters.

gnes walked into Vegan is the New Black and caught sight of a bleary-eyed Deirdre brushing her teeth over a sink the size of an egg cup. Deirdre smiled half-heartedly and wiped her mouth. Spending nights in the storeroom played havoc with her sleep, and if she was honest with herself, it was all wearing a bit thin.

Agnes told her about the panto and her desperate need for a "tan without streaks" that hid "frowns, wobbly skin, and sunspots."

"I have an audition coming up and I want to glow like a young bride," she said.

Deirdre, slipping her toiletries under the basin, listened. It always helped when caught on the hop.

Agnes moved around the shop. She looked at the "living in the present" mandala, the organic soaps shaped as Buddhas, and Deirdre's kind face. She knew she was in the right place.

"Years ago, my principal boy was a given," said Agnes, "and auditions were a mere formality."

Deirdre offered Agnes an herbal tea. She knew all about George and his pantos. He was friends with her ex.

George arrived ten years ago claiming he knew everything about pantomime and could turn the failing audience around. The panto players were excited and arranged a meeting with millionaires short-bread and ginger loaf. George called the meeting a coup. He arrived early and greeted each cast member by their character name from the last panto followed by a quick critique. The only time he smiled was when Agnes, who apparently had stolen the show, arrived.

"George used to love my principal boy," Agnes said to Deirdre. "Not any more, not since my frigging birthday bash. He seems to think I am past it."

She paused, picked up a scented candle, and sniffed. "I need to show them they're wrong. I need to be spectacular for my audition."

Deirdre, placing the candle back on the shelf, muttered a "may I?" and gestured to Agnes's face.

Agnes nodded.

Deirdre touched her cheek. "Your skin just needs a little . . . glow."

"I see, and how much does a glow cost?"

Deirdre talked her through a few of the creams and Agnes's face softened. Then Deirdre offered her a free facial and led her into the storeroom.

Agnes looked at the rolled-up sleeping bag, the clothes neatly hanging from the wall, and the box of vegan Cup-a-Soup on top of the microwave.

"You live here?" she said.

"No," lied Deirdre and gestured to the chair.

Deirdre gave Agnes a luxurious face massage that had Agnes glowing like a woman half her age. And a shoulder massage that took away the pain of a bad night's sleep, a day hunched over a computer fretting. Agnes looked in the mirror; her face glowed. *Even Quasimodo would look good if he had this every day,* she thought . . .

Deirdre gave her some water and touched her shoulders. "You're very tense. I could do more work another time if you like."

Agnes sighed. "That would be heaven. You have no idea what I have to deal with." She looked about the storeroom again, then at the wispy Deirdre. She was as thin as a crisp.

"When was the last time you had a decent meal?" Agnes asked.

Deirdre looked at the microwave.

"Cup-a-Soup is not food. I mean something hot, tasty, and home-cooked."

"I am busy building things up." She shrugged. "It cost more than I thought."

"You do live here, don't you?" said Agnes.

"Yes," said Deirdre, "but hopefully not for long."

When Agnes talked about a free room for free treatments, Deirdre didn't even think, she jumped at the chance—despite what she had heard about "the partner."

Anything was better than another morning skulking to the public toilets.

When the partner Lesley heard, she threw a tantrum and tossed her builder's brew tea in the sink with disgust. She had heard all about the new Vegan is the New Black shop and its owner. The last thing she wanted was some vegan-swilling goody two-shoes moving in. She liked her space and her bacon, and she didn't like sharing Agnes with anyone.

"Why should I give up my study to some organic-loving freak?" she said. "She'll insist on recycled toilet paper, dairy-free cheese, and saving lost cats riddled with ringworm. And who wants to put up with that?"

Agnes, with a laugh she usually kept for her panto performances, ruffled Lesley's short hair. "A bit of vegan would do you good," she said, with a glance at Lesley's round hips.

Lesley tossed another cup into the sink.

"Just joking," said Agnes, playfully tapping her thighs. "I love your luscious hips. They're so earthy, like your sense of humour."

Lesley glared at her partner. *Earthy, I'll give her earthy,* she thought and stomped upstairs.

Lesley had just the right thing for Miss Goody Two-Shoes . . . and made plans to visit her best pal and gamekeeper.

Lesley and Agnes had met a long time ago, in the days when Lesley didn't have to worry about close-up photos for the panto and they begged her to join. Agnes had been a beauty queen, the girl most likely to succeed, and was even married to a very minor celebrity for a while: a DJ who was as straight as she was and, like her, not keen to acknowledge it. Their arrangement lasted as long as the DJ's career: he ended up meeting the love of his life and moving to a farm to breed happy hens, ducks, and pigs with pet names.

Agnes moved back to Lochgilphead, her hometown, and took over her parents' hotel. Lesley was the chef who specialised in game cooking and weird ways of roasting meat outside. Agnes was in her thirties and Lesley was a few years younger.

The first time she saw Lesley she was standing in the kitchen slicing the side of a cow into sirloin and fillet steaks. She watched as Lesley rolled back her sleeves and sharpened the knife before carving . . . the succulent flesh fell from the bone. Back then Lesley's arms were a thing of muscular beauty, glistening under the fluorescent light.

Agnes tasted lust for the first time.

They spent many nights by barbecues, laughing as meat roasted on the embers. In fact, neither Agnes nor Lesley can remember when they stopped having barbecues, probably when the hotel clientele changed from families and couples to bus parties of old people.

Lesley still helped out at the hotel, despite the new owners. She liked keeping her hand in when it came to cooking and the new ways of charging high prices for tiny portions of meat balanced on a smidgen of sauce. She loved cooking as much as gardening and was even happy to help with the odd bus party or wedding do.

Agnes, on the other hand, was more of an old-fashioned book-keeper and still kept her hand in with the odd small business. She was at home over a computer filling in spreadsheets than frying or digging; she liked to keep her hands clean.

3

THE STUDY

Beware the freebie, usually someone else is missing out.

Deirdre arrived late in the afternoon after her Saturday rush. Clutching a yoga mat, a teapot, and an astrology chart, she tentatively knocked at the door.

She had heard about Lesley, the chef with arms like a wrestler. Who could butcher a cow in an afternoon and have all the innards stuffed with sausage meat by nightfall? Whose greatest claim to fame was a haggis peppered with twenty secret spices?

Lesley opened the door and wanted to shut it again. Deirdre was a wispy slip of a girl who looked like she'd struggle to open a crisp packet: just the sort that Agnes liked to take under her wing.

Deirdre stared up at Lesley's six-foot frame and gulped. Lesley looked like she was in the middle of chopping something, and Deirdre, from the state of Lesley's greasy apron, had no intentions of finding out what it was.

"Is Agnes there?" stuttered Deirdre.

Lesley sipped her black builder's tea, finishing with an "Arrrh!"

"It just that she said now was the right time to bring my things," said Deirdre.

"Things?" she sniffed.

"Yes, and . . . and move in."

"Let her in and stop trying to scare her," yelled Agnes from the kitchen. "The spare room's made up."

Lesley, with a tut and good eyeing-over, motioned Deirdre in, took her upstairs, and pushed open a door.

"The spare room," she snapped.

Deirdre stared into the black hole full of shadows of boxes, and what anyone else would call 'a cupboard.'

"In there?" she whispered.

Lesley pulled the light cord illuminating a cubby hole full of shoe-boxes and a rolled-up rug. "Well, yes, what did you expect for nothing?"

Deirdre walked into the cupboard, it was worse than her store-room. She turned to Lesley, now standing arms crossed with a *just say the word and I'll have you* look, when Agnes appeared with a tray of tea.

"You're such a joker," she laughed.

Lesley's stance collapsed as she turned to look at the love of her life with soft eyes.

Agnes gestured to the study across from the cupboard, handed Lesley the tray, ripped the "Lesley's study—enter at your own peril" sign from the door, and pushed it open.

Deirdre shifted with unease and attempted a smile. "You sure about this? I am happy with the cupboard. After all," she feebly joked. "It is a walk-in."

"Exactly," snapped Lesley.

Deirdre blushed.

"Don't be ridiculous," snapped Agnes, and with a 'who pays the bills' look at Lesley she marched into the room.

The other two women followed.

Deirdre gasped . . .

It was a study with a view that brightened even the darkest of karmas and an interior that would chill the liver of a vegan. On one wall was the head of a deer with a variety of leather straps hanging from its antlers. On another were photos of men posing with guns and surrounded by dead birds.

"Where the hell has all this come from?" said Agnes.

"What do you mean?" said Lesley coyly.

"This . . . this . . . hunting nonsense," snapped Agnes.

"I am getting in touch with my earthy side," said Lesley.

Agnes slid Deirdre's yoga mat onto the desk, knocking over a picture of a fox with a glassy-eyed rabbit drooping from its mouth. Lesley picked up the picture with a glare at Deirdre.

"Earthy," said Agnes, "is brown carpet and orange walls, not stuffed animals and guns."

"You have your panto," muttered Lesley, "I have this." She gestured with her hands.

"I don't need a room," muttered Deirdre, "just . . . a place to sleep."

"Since when has all this . . . hunting nonsense been you?" said Agnes. "You can't even stuff a chicken."

Deirdre winced.

"I am a chef, I stuff things all the time. And besides . . . people change," said Lesley.

"Change," said Agnes, "is something you put in your bag."

"I'm happy to sleep anywhere . . . the couch if that's . . . more convenient," muttered Deirdre.

"Not all this . . ." Agnes gestured with her arms, ". . . macabre—er —ly?

"Or the shed," whispered Deidre.

"Nobody is sleeping on the couch," snapped Agnes. "Or the shed, for Christ's sake."

Lesley glared at her so-called soul mate. "Well, that's what you think," she snapped and stomped out.

Lesley, fed up with the whole "sharing" thing, moaned as Deirdre moved in. And as Deirdre tried to make herself at home, Lesley tried to intimidate.

Deirdre had instincts finely tuned from years of "natural" therapies. She could read people like she could read tea leaves, and what she read from Lesley was hatred on a par with her ex. In fact, Lesley was just like her ex: a man used to people jumping to attention.

Deirdre's hands were soon shaking again like they used to whenever she heard her ex's trademark cough.

It was a shake that broke things. When she dropped and broke his Winchester 49, Malcom raged. And it was not long after that that Malcolm, after a vicious attack on her cookery books, walked out of her life forever . . .

After a week, Lesley had taken to growling, "If that damn panto did her head in, then that wimpy Deirdre did her nut in . . ."

Agnes laughed, soothed, and head-ruffled, none of which helped but rather exasperated Lesley even more.

"How long is she staying?" Lesley moaned one morning.

Agnes sighed over her coffee. "Long? What do you mean? Look at her. She's a great help, don't know why you're so anti."

Lesley stared out of the kitchen window. Deirdre was hanging out the washing; flapping like a two-man tent was her *comfy* underwear, dwarfing Deirdre's frilly egg cup bra and knickers.

Deirdre had hips the size of a marathon runner and underwear the size of a facecloth. Lesley's ample curves, however, required firmer attention, underwear that held, lifted, and separated; in short, her bra could easily hold a watermelon.

Lesley had never been good at sticking to things, especially diets. And it's not like she didn't try. She roasted vegetables with every seed going, grilled chops with not even a hint of fat, but she always wanted something afterwards, something sweet, dairy-loaded, and moreish.

Deirdre, on the other hand, didn't touch cream and could say no to a cake with a chuckle. In fact, she chuckled nervously at everything, which not only set Lesley's teeth on edge but stopped her cracking jokes of any kind.

Lesley huffed. "Must she do that?"

"What?"

"Hang my smalls . . ." Her voice died away.

"You do like your sweets, my little cupcake," said Agnes.

Lesley stared at Agnes, glowing like a spring chicken from Deirdre's morning organic facial, and huffed. "Must you?"

"What?"

"Glow like that? Especially in the morning. I prefer you more groggy and croaky," lied Lesley.

The truth was, the love of her life looked amazing . . . *and it was all thanks to that frigging vegan.*

A PAIR OF LEGGINGS

Pleasure without pain. If only.

Over the next few weeks, things went from bad to seriously bad. Lesley retreated to the lounge sulking in front of the TV, while Agnes took up all of Deirdre's time.

Deirdre anxiously worried. She was not the sort of woman to want to come between a couple; she was more a peacemaker. And as she oiled, rubbed, and kneaded Agnes's body, she wondered what could soften the heart of such an Amazonian woman.

One Saturday night, as Deirdre worked on a tough knot in Agnes's shoulder, she caught sight of Lesley flashing past the kitchen window. They were sitting by the Agar at the time, Agnes's face plastered in Deirdre's much-talked-about charcoal-and-clay mask. Agnes, mulling over why she hadn't heard anything about the auditions, mumbled something about "a bit late in the day," followed by a grimace, a yelp, and an "ahhh" as Deirdre pressed into her flesh.

She fluttered her eyes shut . . .

"Bliss."

Lesley passed the window again, this time pushing a wheelbarrow full of wood like it was as light as a chocolate box.

Deirdre stopped to watch . . .

What she wouldn't give for a Lesley-free day, a day when she could go to bed without hanging something over that god-awful stuffed deer head, or even better, move into her own flat.

An axe clattered to the ground. Lesley picked it up and tossed it back into the wheelbarrow like it was a toothpick.

Deirdre hated Lesley with more venom than a tub of lard. Deirdre, however, was also an idealist, a pacifist, and a realist, and getting on with Lesley the meat-eating giant would make her life so much easier.

Lesley wiped her mouth, looked up, caught Deirdre's eye, ignored her weak smile, and moved on.

"What about a wax . . . about the lips," muttered Deirdre. "It might make a difference."

"What?" said Agnes who had retreated into her imaginary panto world of leather, boots, and applause.

"Or maybe a deep tissue sort of thing about the legs—get rid of some of that fluid."

Agnes's eyes flashed open. "Fluid, I don't have any fluid, especially on my legs. They are my best bit. George says my legs are so fabulous they should be insured."

"I was talking about Lesley," muttered Deirdre.

"Oh."

"Maybe a free treatment would warm her up a bit, win her over."

Lesley passed the window again, this time with a chainsaw.

"She's not that sort of a girl," said Agnes. "She is unwinnable, and that is what I love about her."

"It's just that she's a bit off-putting . . ." said Deirdre. (She scared the crap out of her.) "Especially in the morning."

"Nonsense."

"She stands at the kettle and growls," said Deirdre, "blocking the tea cupboard. I haven't had a herbal in weeks."

"Don't be ridiculous," sighed Agnes. "My Lesley's a pussycat."

Deirdre stared into the garden watching Lesley oil the chainsaw. *That woman has the strength of an ox.* She smiled nervously. Her stomach squeezed and churned. She had never been a cat person. It was the whole bringing a dead bird/mouse thing as a present. It gave her the shivers.

"What about a colonic flush then? For all that anger?"

"If she's not letting you near the kettle, I hardly think she's going to let you down below."

Agnes settled back in her chair and closed her eyes. "Leave her to me." She patted Deirdre's hand. "Treat 'em mean, keep 'em keen, that's what I say, always works with my pussycat."

Deirdre had her doubts; after all, "treat 'em mean, keep 'em keen" is what her ex used to say. She poured more oil onto her hands and watched Lesley peel off her shirt.

Deirdre stopped . . .

Lesley in a vest was larger than ever. She looked like a wrestler gone to seed. Her once-muscular arms wobbled, her large round hips burst over her camouflage pants, and her hands were like shovels.

Deirdre watched as Lesley with one almighty pull revved the chainsaw into action, manoeuvring it like it was a set of straighteners.

The noise filled the kitchen.

Agnes jumped. "Christ almighty, what's she up to now?"

She banged on the window.

Lesley, attacking the bottom of a tree with gusto, didn't hear.

Agnes opened the window, shouted something obscene, shut it again, and without a passing glance at Deirdre marched into the garden, oblivious to the tissue paper flying from her collar.

Agnes tapped Lesley's shoulder; Lesley jumped with a squeal, and the chainsaw clattered to the ground sounding like a cow drowning in slow motion.

Lesley stared at Agnes's painted white face and began to laugh.

Deirdre watched without hearing as Agnes gestured like an irate referee.

Lesley cried with laughter.

Agnes continued to shout.

Lesley gestured to her ear.

Agnes shouted louder. "Will . . . frigging . . ."

Tissue paper fluttered onto the chainsaw; it squealed like an electrocuted cat.

Lesley shut the saw off.

". . . ARSE!!!"

. . .

Deirdre handed Agnes a soothing cup of camomile and her soul mate a robust builder's tea. Agnes sipped while Lesley slurped followed by an "arrrrh" designed to rile Agnes.

"Must you drink like a plumber?" croaked Agnes, her throat still sore from the shouting.

"Arrrrr . . ."

Deirdre looked at Lesley's arms glistening in the kitchen light. She was still chirpy. Deirdre took a chance. "You fancy a rub?" She nodded towards the oils.

Lesley choked on her tea. "Me a rub from you?"

"Why not?"

"She's not a rubbing kind," said Agnes.

"What?"

"Massage is not your thing," said Agnes.

"How would you know?"

"I always know."

"I might like a rub with a bit of oil," said Lesley.

"I know you like the back of my hand," said Agnes.

"Know? Hardly. You don't even know there's another woman in the running for the principal boy, do you?"

Agnes, choking on her tea, recovered quickly. "What are you on about?"

"And she's half your age," said Lesley.

As Agnes steadied herself by the agar, Lesley lifted her mug to a safer place.

"Her name is Lucinda and she's an entertainer," said Lesley.

Lucinda worked in the Argyll as, to quote the postman, "chief cook and bottle washer" as well as an entertainer. Apparently, she could turn her hand to anything.

She was twenty, single, wore shorts at the drop of a hat, and, according to the postman, was a pole dancer so flexible she could suck her big toe.

George had walked in on her mopping the floor in shorts so high he forgot what he came in for. And now, so the postman claimed, she was working on a new script with a principal boy contortionist which would pull in the crowds and pack the hall.

Agnes's desperation was now at a fever pitch. And for the next week, Deirdre and Agnes took up yoga in the sitting room in an effort to expand Agnes's leg kick while Lesley watched, confident they were wasting their time.

Did they seriously think a spot of yoga could compete?

"Deirdre's taking the piss. There is as much chance of you beating Lucinda as me tucking into tofu," said Lesley, grabbing the TV remote.

"Piss?" said Agnes. "Deirdre understands me and my dreams, you're the one taking the piss."

Lesley let out a long sigh and flopped on the couch. She stared at her soul mate mid eagle pose, then flicked on the TV.

"How long are you going to be?"

"As long as it takes."

"You are putting me off Celebrity Chef."

"You hate Celebrity Chef," snapped Agnes.

Lesley turned up the volume as a young chef robustly stuffed a guinea fowl with haggis.

Deirdre began to gag.

"Must you?" said Agnes.

"Must I?" said Lesley with a *dare you* raised eyebrow.

Agnes flicked the TV off at the switch, then matched Lesley's raised eyebrow with a glare.

Deirdre raced to the bathroom.

"What has happened to you?" said Agnes.

"What do you mean?"

"Where's my little comedian? That funny girl I used to live with?"

Deirdre began to retch. *Lesley, a comedian?*

"These days you're as depressing as rain at a funeral," said Agnes.

"What do you expect? You have as much time for me as Miss Muffet has for meat. You sniff at me like a dog at a bowl of week-old chum."

"I do not."

"The only thing you're interested in is how high you and Miss"—she gestured with the remote—"Muffet can get your legs."

Deirdre stared down at the toilet bowl. She pulled at the toilet paper and wiped her mouth.

Then she remembered the answering machine and Lesley playing it back.

5

THE TEAPOT

A size ten is only a number.

When Agnes arrived at the first panto players' rehearsal, her ready-for-battle entrance silenced the room. No one thought she was coming.

Dressed in her leather jeans and matching jacket, she greeted George with a gloved handshake, held a pose for everyone to see her tight new yoga arse, then took a seat beside Heather, the secretary, publicists, and coffee maker.

George stood at the back of the hall and ordered the lights "dimmed" and a spotlight for Derek turned on.

The postman, poised on a ladder sorting the lighting, shouted, "Hold your horses," which George ignored, switching the main lights off.

The hall plunged into dark silence as the cast waited for Derek to appear onstage.

Derek stood at the side of the stage praying for an electrical catastrophe. The dress was so bad he couldn't even summon up the courage to look in the mirror.

The postman continued to manipulate the spotlight, it flashed across the hall catching George mid nose pick.

"Whoops . . ." said the postman.

George, fumbling for his megaphone, shouted "Jesus man, the stage . . ."

Derek blinked into the spotlight. Then, after a failed saunter, limped onto centre stage an apparition of pink taffeta that had the cast gasping. Many had seen the dress hanging in the dressing room, but none were prepared for the sight of it on a man with one leg shorter than the other.

"Jesus," muttered a voice from the back.

"Who the hell made that?" said Agnes.

Heather nodded towards an uncomfortable-looking Deloris.

Derek attempted a shoe shuffle, knocked over the cardboard cutout wolf, and winced. George turned up his megaphone.

Agnes felt for Derek. She had tried to teach him tap-dancing, and she had taught many reluctant dancers, but Derek defeated her. He had as much interest in tap dance as Lesley had in pantomime. It was Catrina, his mother, who pushed him, along with the stupid idea that dancing to Rod Stewart songs would be a hoot with the audience.

Rod Stewart had as much to do with pantomime as garden furniture. And Derek, as she pointed out to Catrina, was as funny as a runny nose. Not that Catrina listened; in fact, it was only after a run-in with Lesley that Catrina backed off from the tap-dancing lessons.

"Poor bastard," muttered Agnes as he finally left.

Heather said nothing. She knew what was coming next.

George with a blasting nose-blow into his hankie walked up onto the stage, looked about the cast, and clapped his hands for attention.

He passed around the new *Little Red Riding Hood* script, written by Charlie, a writer who had never written anything before apart from a mildly funny short story about Santa's G-string.

"As you can see, there are a few changes," said George.

"What?" said a voice from the back.

"Not you." George turned to Agnes. "The principals."

"You mean like Derek."

"No, not Derek," he muttered with a sigh.

Agnes flipped through the script. Where her name should be was Lucinda's. She looked up. "What the hell is this?"

"The new script."

"But the principal boy?"

"Yes . . ."

"It's always me. I have fans who come to see me every year."

"Well if they do, it's not filling the hall. We hardly broke even last year," said Heather.

"We need something new, different," said George.

"My interpretations *are* different. They're unique." Agnes looked about the blank faces. No one said anything; it was like they already knew.

"What about the auditions?" said Agnes.

"Done and dusted," said George.

"What? But I have been preparing, stretching, and . . ."

"You never turned up," said Heather.

"I knew nothing about it."

"It doesn't matter, we have our cast."

"Lucinda? But she mops floors."

"She sings in a tribute band," said the postman climbing down from his ladder, "even has a following."

"And a Facebook page," said Heather, flicking on the kettle.

"Have you seen what she does?" said Agnes. "Impressions of singers from the sixties and she has no idea about costuming. I mean silver hot pants? Since when did the likes of Paul McCartney wear silver?'

"I've never heard any complaints," said the same annoying voice from the back.

"Her impressions," said Agnes, "stretch the imagination more than those hot pants of hers stretch across her backside.'

"She fills the bar every Saturday night," said George.

"That's because there's free pizza after midnight," said Agnes.

"And the hot pants," said the voice from the back.

Agnes threw him a glare.

"It is time for you to explore other talents," said Heather, plonking a milky coffee in front of her. "We all have to move on sometimes and wee ones don't want to see the principal boy collecting her pension in the post office the next day."

"No one collects their pension anymore," said Agnes. She threw Heather a dirty look. She still hadn't forgiven her for the illustration on the last program. Heather had drawn her with more wrinkles than a deflated balloon left out in the sun.

"I could be your fairy then, I'm still a size ten."

"Filled."

Agnes looked around.

"The gym teacher," said Heather, describing an audition to beat all auditions. "She minced in a tutu like a hippo wearing stilettos—it was hilarious." She laughed.

"But she's so loud, and she's built like a tank. Now you can't tell me *she* has a following," said Agnes.

No one said anything; watching Agnes's demise was as painful as watching a mouse zigzag from a cat: pointless, exhausting, and, in the end, futile.

"I think," said George in a quiet tone, "it's time for you to consider something more . . . behind the scenes."

"I am happy to try the narrator?" said Agnes.

"Filled," said George.

Agnes looked about questioningly.

"The district nurse," said the postman.

"But she's South African."

"She auditioned," said George. He nodded to Charlie the writer. "And Charlie here has written a speech perfect for her accent."

Agnes tutted. *What the hell has this pantomime come to?*

The cast shifted uncomfortably as Heather cracked open a packet of digestives.

In the end, Agnes was offered the part of the singing teapot. News she took in a tight-lipped fashion.

6

THE AUDITION

Wanting too much can lead to a missed opportunity.

When Agnes arrived home, the first person she told was Lesley. Lesley was standing on their patio staring out onto the loch lapping in the wind. The waves were high and often crashed onto the carpark below by the community hall.

"They didn't even tell me about the auditions," she muttered.

"Did they not?" said Lesley sheepishly.

"He said he had."

"Hmmm."

"I feel like a fool," muttered Agnes.

"Maybe now you'll listen to me," said Lesley, tossing a crust at a seagull.

Deirdre walked onto the patio carrying three large gins. "The teapot's got some good lines," she said. "And you've got the legs for it."

"There is more to life than soya and panto," muttered Lesley with a cold look at Deirdre.

"And I heard the outfit is pretty impressive," said Deirdre.

"A teapot? Impressive? What you on?" said Lesley with an aggressive toss of bread. The seagull squawked.

Agnes tipped all three gins into one glass and downed it. In her eyes, the whole cast was in on it.

"They always told me about the auditions." She crunched on her ice. "Not this time."

"Just say no," said Lesley. "You don't have to do it."

"I am in one scene," said Agnes. "Just *one*." She pulled a face. "The singing garden furniture scene." She looked at her empty glass. "Deck chairs . . . in a panto. What next? A barbecue with dancing sausages, a fried onion chorus?"

"Tell 'em to stuff it," said Lesley, topping up Agnes's glass.

"I mean since when did Little Red Riding Hood have garden furniture?" said Agnes.

"I heard it's funny," said Deirdre.

"Funny? That frigging Charlie has written me a part that could make me the biggest joke Lochgilphead has seen in years." She emptied her glass and looked out onto the loch. "And George thinks it's a hoot! Told me to start collecting cardboard boxes."

The seagull dived across the water and over the patio, leaving a dropping on the floor.

"'It's a great part,' he said, 'made for you, you don't even need to audition.'" Agnes sighed. "Who's he kidding? I heard no one showed up for the teapot auditions."

Deirdre offered to soothe Agnes with a deluxe Hawaiian massage that not only took two hours but would leave her feeling detached from her past, and hopefully floaty.

The room was warm, the table covered in a shag pile towel on par with the fur of a Persian cat. Deirdre told her to strip, lay facedown on the table, and cover herself with a sari. Agnes slid her face into the hole at the top of the table and began to mumble.

"That Charlie's got a lot to answer for," she muttered. "One chorus, that's all I have. I mean the deck chairs have more character than I have."

The Hawaiian music started. Agnes closed her eyes then opened them and turned to Deirdre.

"Don't know who they are dealing with."

"Shhh . . ."

"I trained with the best."

Deirdre eased Agnes back into position.

Agnes sprung up. "Molly Mudgen's Taptastic School."

"Just lie down and relax."

"I even taught dance before I came to this hole of a place."

Deirdre eased Agnes back into position and rearranged her hair to one side.

"Tried to teach that Derek," Agnes muttered through the hole. "Maybe that was my mistake."

Deloris fluttered the sari across her body. "Just breathe count to four and . . ."

"Garden furniture-played by school children-haven't a frigging clue."

". . . relax, the past is the past."

"I mean what am I a pair of legs . . ."

"Close your eyes . . . clear your mind."

"To poke out of any stupid costume they can think of?"

"Annnnd . . . think of something nice . . ."

Agnes felt a soft hand adjust her head back into place followed by warm oil on her back. Deirdre pushed into her flesh and down her body with the inside of her lower arm.

Agnes closed her eyes, muttered "frigging panto," then drifted into another place: Panto land, where she was young and gay and Lesley was cheering her on.

Deirdre moved up and down her body in swift moves. Agnes floated across the stage in dark stockings and stilettos, her heels clipping the boards in a dance . . .

Deirdre's hands revolved her feet, moved up the soles, her legs, and back to her head.

Agnes tossed her hat into the audience, they cheered . . . the music stopped.

"What the hell is this?" snapped Lesley.

Deirdre looked up. "It's Hawaiian. I can give you one if you want."

"What are you, a pervert? One not enough?"

Agnes, confused, looked up, tissue paper sticking to her face. She focused on Lesley.

"It's a massage," said Deirdre.

"She's naked," said Lesley.

"Naked?" said Agnes. "Who's naked? I was dancing." She rubbed her eyes to waken.

"She's not naked," said Deirdre, gesturing to the disposable G-string.

"That tissue paper of a thing doesn't even hide her latest waxing."

"Don't be ridiculous," Agnes said, spitting tissue from her lips. "We are all girls here."

"I am always ridiculous to you."

Agnes wrapped a towel about her and sat up.

"That's because you do ridiculous things."

"Me, I'm not the one killing myself to beat a girl young enough to be my granddaughter."

Agnes jumped up and followed Lesley as she left the room.

"There is more talent in my little finger than that whole sad excuse of an impersonator."

"But they don't think so, do they?"

Agnes's face crumbled.

Lesley's face softened. "Just as well you didn't audition. I saved you the humiliation."

"What?"

"You should be grateful."

"Grateful?"

Deirdre, spying yet another fallout, discreetly left, as Lesley told Agnes, "It was for your own good."

Agnes argued with Lesley until Lesley, tearful, left and Agnes, angry, stomped.

Lesley, deleting the audition message, had sent Agnes into a spin of yelling that went on for ages. Lesley didn't get a word in and finally left muttering about *it* being "all over for good."

Agnes, enraged about the message and ignoring the "for good" comment, decided to prove her partner wrong. And spent several hours in her room looking at her legs in the mirror, along with the teapot design Deloris had given her.

Up till then, she had been thinking about tossing the whole teapot thing in. But now, thanks to Lesley interfering, she was angry and wanted to make Lesley eat her words.

A few weeks later, Agnes had not only come to terms with but embraced her new *character role* with a selection of sparkling stockings and a repertoire of teapot voices. She was in the middle of performing her latest creations to Deirdre and a bored Lesley, when Heather appeared.

She arrived through the kitchen door to find Agnes in sparkling stockings with a TV cardboard box around her middle singing, "*I'm a little teapot short and stout . . .*"

Lesley with a long face offered her tea or "something stronger."

Heather, after dipping her digestive into the something stronger, told the three women about the planned emergency meeting.

"He is planning to surprise Herself."

"Who?" said Deirdre.

"Catrina," said Lesley.

"She wants to take over: new script," said Heather.

"New script?" said Agnes. "I didn't know there was one."

"Did you not?" said Lesley innocently.

"Nobody tells me anything," said Agnes with a caustic look at Lesley.

"He has this idea," said Heather, "for a chase scene and a chiminea —full flamed."

"Full flamed? On stage?" Lesley blew threw her teeth. "Bit dicey."

Heather eyed Agnes's cardboard box. "That's what the postman said."

"If that thing goes up, so will the hall," said Lesley. Like a mine field —a gas leak."

"That also what the postman," said Heather.

"Hiroshima here we come," said Lesley, topping up her gin.

"George is obsessed with putting Herself in her place."

"Catrina?" Deirdre looked at Agnes again. Agnes nodded while negotiating the kitchen stool.

Heather eyed Agnes as she tried to manipulate her box above her waistline while arranging her hips on the stool. "He wants to try it out at the emergency meeting."

The stool crashed to the ground; Heather picked it up.

"The dancing deck chair scene," said Heather.

"With a chiminea —full flamed?" said Lesley.

Heather nodded.

"There's no way you're going to that . . . in that." Lesley gestured to the box. "You may as well chuck an oily rag on your head, light up a spliff, and say your prayers."

"Spliff?" said Deirdre.

Lesley looked at her with a *seriously* face.

"There's no need to be so dramatic," said Agnes.

"She's right," muttered Deirdre.

Lesley coughed on her. "Something stronger."

"George has gone loopy," said Deirdre.

"What is he, a breakfast cereal?" muttered Lesley.

"Saw him at Tesco," said Deirdre, "rolling lighters in his hands and chuckling."

"That Catrina tipped him over the edge," said Heather.

The others nodded. They had heard about Catrina standing up to George, toppling his megaphone.

"She called Charlie a hack. Apparently, she read 'Santa's G-string' and said it was as funny as a nosebleed."

Lesley topped up the gin, adding some ice.

"If I were you," said Heather, "I'd give the rehearsals a miss."

7

THE BLACK FOREST GATEAU

Loyalty is easily forgotten.

It was Lesley who first saw the fire; she was standing on the patio with a perfect view of the community hall. She had just plopped ice into her gin and was toying with the idea of slicing a lemon when she looked up to see a stream of smoke billowing from a window.

She sipped. "Agnes . . ."

Agnes, planted by the Agar with Deirdre massaging a geranium oil blend into her skin, did not move.

"This meeting of yours," said Lesley, "what time was it?"

Deirdre circled Agnes's temples . . .

"Arrrh," muttered Agnes.

"Is it still in the community hall?" said Lesley. She looked at her glass, then added more gin.

Agnes looked up. "Yes, why?"

"Come and see this."

Deirdre moved down to Agnes's jawline.

"Just tell me," muttered Agnes.

Lesley watched as the cast spilled out from the hall. "You better come and see for yourself. There's smoke for miles."

Flames burst the glass in the window—

"Seriously, words can't explain . . ."

—followed by a loud bang from inside the hall.

Agnes jumped. "Jesus."

Deirdre raced out to the balcony followed by Agnes.

They watched motionlessly as flames licked around the edges of other windows. The fire engine arrived, followed by shouting and hose pulling.

Lesley drained her glass, poured another, and put a protective arm around her partner. "That could have been you, dearest . . . drink?"

"Thank God for the geranium," muttered Deirdre, who had kept Agnes waiting an hour while she searched for it.

They watched as Deloris emerged, shaken. Then she was engulfed by a paramedic with a blanket, followed by what they assumed was George on a trolley and Charlie clutching scenery as he staggered.

"Jesus," said Agnes again.

"What's he clutching?" said Deirdre.

"Who cares," said Lesley, handing her partner a gin. Agnes shook her head; Lesley tipped it into her glass. "Let's just celebrate that you—my love—were not there."

"It's a headless Dick . . ." said Agnes.

"Excuse me?" said Deirdre.

". . . Whittington," finished Agnes. "The postman's finest . . . what a gentleman."

"That's that," said Lesley, guzzling her gin.

"I mean who would do that? Think of the postman," muttered Agnes.

"What you on about?" said Deirdre.

"No more George, no more hall," said Lesley with a smack of lips.

"He loved that piece," said Agnes. "It was the first thing he ever made for the panto players."

"It's made of cardboard," said Deirdre.

"No more panto," said Lesley, "no more recording *Strictly*. We can now watch it live." She chuckled to herself.

Agnes looked at the love of her life. "How much have you had?"

Lesley pulled a face, then drained her glass.

"You panto people are weird," muttered Deirdre.

"Tell me about it," said Lesley, refilling her glass.

Catrina took over the panto, and within days, a new script arrived at Agnes's door, along with a note . . .

"There will always be a panto. Because in this sad world, sometimes a woman dressed as a man is all we have."

Lesley picked up the package, ripped it open, held her breath, and prayed. Then, she rejoiced. It was the worst script she had ever seen. Agnes's part was minuscule with a teapot design more like a tea urn covering her best bits: her legs. Lesley couldn't wait to show Agnes and hear the words, "Me, in that? As if."

"Who does she think she is," muttered Agnes dumping the script in the bin. "I have no time for that woman," she said patting Lesley's hips, "she is a right pain in the bahoochie."

Agnes put away her stockings and the teapot designs and made herself at home in front of the TV.

Deirdre, with a sense of relief, began to make plans to find a home. She was no longer needed for the daily massages, and her shop, thanks to Agnes's "her creams work miracles" comments to everyone she met, was doing OK.

Lesley cheered up, made plans for a walking holiday, and bought tickets to the *Strictly Come Dancing* show in Glasgow. She even offered to help Deirdre look for a flat.

Peace rained on the Agnes and Lesley household; they had even taken to holding hands in front of Strictly repeats, until a week later when Catrina offered Agnes the principal boy.

Lucinda, with her "I've taken up pole dancing" excuse, had resigned. She, along with the district nurse, were the first of many to drop out. No one wanted to work with Catrina. Even the salsa dancers who would dance at the drop of a hat had found another gig.

Catrina was as popular as anthrax.

"Looks like teaching Derek has earned me a few brownie points?" muttered Agnes, flicking through the script.

"You can't be serious," said Lesley, "after what that cow put you through, I mean don't you remember?"

"Yes, but I am a principal boy again."

"In a script that is as funny as the news night. I mean look at this, how is a dame in a green onesie funny?"

"It could be."

"Derek in a green onesie? I hardly think so."

"Who cares about Derek?"

"George is like a genius compared to her, at least some of his ideas worked."

"But she chose me to play the principal boy—no audition."

Lesley looked at her. *Is she serious?*

"She said she always loved my Dick Whittington, and I'm a perfect fit for the size-ten costume." Agnes smiled.

Lesley gave up. She went into the drawer, pulled out the *Strictly Come Dancing* tickets, and phoned to cancel. *What was the point? Agnes had the memory of an ant and the loyalty of a ravenous dog.*

Agnes didn't notice, she'd left the room, but Deirdre did. She watched as Lesley ripped the *Strictly Come Dancing* tickets to pieces and tossed them into the bin, her thick arms shaking with emotion. She wanted to shout at her lover, remind her of all that Catrina had put her through, but it was pointless.

"The whole tap-dancing saga conventionally forgotten," she muttered. "Thanks to a crappy part in a rubbish panto." She looked at Deirdre. "It was me who sorted things."

"So I heard," said Deirdre. *Who hadn't?*

"With a Black Forest gateau," said Lesley.

And an audience, thought Deirdre.

A few years ago, Lesley was cooking for Catrina and a few of her workmates at the hotel. Lesley, fed up listening to Agnes moan about teaching Derek was in a rage. She marched to the top of the table where Catrina sat and threatened to dye her hair a creamy Black Forest gateau if she didn't stop insisting on the "useless Derek tap-dancing classes." The staff, half cut on cocktails and wine, laughed their heads off as Catrina, sober and stiff, was for the first time speechless.

Agnes's gratitude lasted for weeks; she cooked and nurtured her soul mate, they ate toasted marshmallows by the fire, and giggled over too much gin.

Lesley sighed.

"Now she's best buddies with that woman."

"It won't last," said Deirdre. "You wait and see."

Lesley had her doubts. For the first time ever, Lesley looked at her lover and thought, *What did I see in her?*

8

THE GLASGOW BUS

When one door closes, get on a bus.

*L*esley watched as Agnes prepared for her first meeting with the wonderful Catrina. Agnes's change of heart was a hard blow . . . all the love she had given Agnes seemed tossed aside like a takeaway packet. Ignoring Agnes's glee, Lesley retreated into herself.

It hurt so much . . .

While Agnes left for her first meeting with Catrina and Deirdre left to work in her shop, Lesley remained at home packing her bags. She told herself she was only taking what she brought when she moved in and then, realising it had been over twenty years, burst into tears.

After using up half a roll of toilet paper to wipe her nose, Lesley pulled herself together. She slipped her "over-sixty free" bus pass into her back pocket, her chef whites into a rucksack and walked into the community hall.

No one saw her enter.

She stood in the dark at the back of the hall, silently watching Agnes dance in front of Catrina.

Should she say goodbye, create a scene?

She looked at Agnes's beaming face and a tear ran down her face. Agnes looked so happy . . .

Lesley checked her watch; the Glasgow bus was leaving in ten minutes.

She sighed and left.

"Single, no return," she mumbled to the bus driver. "I'm heading for the Glasgow nightlife."

He looked at her sad face and said, "And when you find it, hen, let me know."

Lesley didn't even answer.

Deirdre arrived home, poured herself a coffee, and stood out on the balcony. Her business had taken off; everyone wanted the "Agnes glow." Deirdre, now earning enough to think of her own place, had found a flat she could afford. She smiled to herself: a home at last. She stared out onto the street below and caught sight of Lesley heading into the community hall with a rucksack on her back.

She watched as Lesley emerged, shoulders slumped, face downcast. Then when she saw Lesley walk onto the Glasgow bus, Deirdre's stomach turned.

She went back to the note in the hall and this time read it . . .

After the rehearsal, Agnes slipped into Tesco's, perusing the sparkling wine section. She could not wait to show Lesley her new dance, in her new leggings. Clutching three bottles of bubbly and a box of celebrations, Agnes jumped into the car and sped off to her soul mate.

Agnes arrived home, dumped her sparkly pair of leggings in the hall, and stared at the mirror. Lesley's "I'm leaving you because you don't give a toss" note stared back. She peeled it off as Deirdre walked in. "You OK?" Deirdre muttered.

"She says she has places to go and people to drink with and if I wasn't prepared to join her, well, she would find someone who damn well would."

Agnes looked at Deirdre.

"She's sixty. Who the hell has a nightlife at sixty?"

"At least I can have my tea in the morning," Deirdre muttered flatly.

"Twenty years just like that, for what? Someone to drink with?"

"And . . . you can toss out that stuffed deer head." Deirdre tried to sound cheerful.

Agnes's face crumpled. "Who will tell me my stance is wrong, my interpretation is not up to par? How am I to perform without her? Who's going to sort out Catrina?"

"I thought you liked Catrina."

"I mean she's already questioning the whole deck chair scene. I had this idea for a tap dance on the table, like this . . ."

Deirdre watched as Agnes sprang into a shoe shuffle, feigning an "I don't give a toss" laugh, then burst into tears.

Lesley's note fluttered to the floor.

Deirdre picked up the note, then poured Agnes a gin.

"Perhaps we'd better leave the deer head," she said. "For when she is back." She sighed; she hadn't the heart to mention the new flat.

A week later, Agnes was still setting a place at the table for Lesley . . . and Deirdre was beginning to worry. In one week, Agnes had turned from a woman with a strut to a "gutted" wreck who believed survival without her "soulmate" was as plausible as her scaling a pole to dance. Agnes had stopped waxing and started wallowing taking on the role of a wounded, abandoned woman with more drama than soap opera.

Every day Agnes stood in the same space as Lesley—blocking the tea cupboard—moaning. She whined to Deirdre about what a "fool she had been," and how the "treat 'em mean and keep 'em keen" approach was a crock of shit.

She constantly made Lesley's favourite food, and then, refusing to eat it, plonked herself in front of recordings of *Strictly* while staring at Lesley's empty chair, crying over the remote, "I am nothing without her."

No one was allowed to sit on Lesley's chair; even the cat was shooed off.

Deirdre spent her time consoling Agnes. She tried everything, from flower essence to Hawaiian massage. She even tried talking to Agnes about living in the present, letting go of the past.

"That Buddhist stuff is a crock of shit," said Agnes. "Living in the present . . . how can you live in the present when the past clings to you like a bad fart?"

Then when Agnes heard about Deirdre's new flat she cried so hard her eyes looked like red golf balls.

"You can't leave," she said, "not now I am on my own. All I have is the stuffed deer to keep me company. How will I manage?"

Deirdre was fed up; she felt trapped. How could she leave a woman who had given her a place to stay when she was so low? She would have been better off staying in the store cupboard than putting up with all this drama. Then, when Agnes missed her rehearsal, Deirdre's panic spun into overdrive. She had to do something, or she'd be stuck with Agnes forever.

She needed a plan.

9

LEMSIP

A cold shared is a cold doubled.

When the panto rebellion happened, Agnes didn't notice; she had no interest. She was in the midst of a cold and dealing with her own Lemsip crisis, lamenting the loss of Lesley's magic touch.

"Lesley knew what to do," she sighed. "Now I must make do—do it all myself."

"It's only pouring from a kettle," said Deirdre. She caught Agnes's look. "And opening a sachet."

Agnes huffed, coughed, and took her Lemsip to bed with as much interest in the rebellion as life itself. Agnes had been offered the fairy godmother role and a chance to do a dance with the deck chairs that, to quote Charlie, "would steal the show." She didn't even look at the script; instead, she tossed it aside, spluttering "I'll think about it," and with a dramatic coughing fit slipped back to bed. Deirdre followed with Vicks VapoRub.

The panto rebellion was a rebellion like no other . . .

Catrina, ousted by her son, didn't know what hit her. Derek had mobilised the cast into action, uniting the moaning fractions with a "we will not take any more" motto and a new revised script. A script that promised laughter, an audience queuing at the doors . . . and Lucinda not only back onstage but using her pole dancing skills.

A week later, Derek arrived at the door with Heather. He wanted to know how the fairy godmother was, to see if she liked the new script and whether she was coming to the rehearsal.

Deirdre answered the door. She had just finished in her shop and the smell of ylang-ylang wafted from her as she opened. Derek looked at the thin wisp of a girl, stopped, and inhaled. It was the last thing he expected to see at Agnes's door.

Heather, throwing Derek a look, asked how Agnes was.

"She could be better," Deirdre muttered.

They heard a cough from upstairs followed by a "Tell them to go away" from Agnes.

Deirdre pulled a face.

"What about the rehearsal?" shouted Heather.

"Leave me be!" Agnes shouted back followed by an exaggerated hacking cough.

"Still no Lesley?" muttered Derek.

"No," said Deirdre.

"Oh, for heaven's sake," muttered Heather. "A few weeks ago, you were moaning about your audience." She shouted, "How the panto could not go on without you—'pivotal' you called yourself."

"So?" shouted Agnes.

"Well isn't that a reason to get out of bed?" shouted Heather. She tutted.

"No," said Agnes followed by a volley of coughs.

"We bent over backwards—created a part just for you," said Heather.

"Who gives a toss," said Agnes.

"I'm coming up," shouted Heather.

"Don't," wailed Agnes, "I've no makeup on."

"I've seen you before," snapped Heather. "And believe me, makeup makes no difference."

"How dare you," sniffed Agnes.

Derek looked at Deirdre. "You run the Vegan is the New Black shop, don't you?"

She nodded with a smile.

"That shop smells like heaven."

Heather thumped up the stairs. "A bit of lippy, a gin or two, and you'll be right as . . ." She burst into Agnes's bedroom. Heather stared at the apparition in the bed, the red golf ball eyes, the red nose, and the pile of used tissues surrounding Agnes's puffy face.

"Jesus . . ."

"Told you I was sick," muttered Agnes. She sipped her Lemsip, coughed, then gagged.

"You look like Miss Piggy," said Heather.

Derek and Deirdre smiled at each other.

"I've heard about your massages," he said. "You should come to the rehearsal, I'm sure a few would benefit from a neck rub."

"Miss Piggy . . . I feel worse than that," said Agnes.

"You have a cold," shouted Heather.

"I'm dying . . ." muttered Agnes.

Heather sucked in her breath.

". . . of a broken heart," wailed Agnes. "Gin will never touch my lips again."

Heather, with several more what-do-I-do-now sighs, finally gave up and thumped back downstairs. She looked from Derek to Deirdre.

"That woman is a lost cause. And I swear there is gin in that Lemsip."

Derek's eyes twinkled at Deirdre as a loud cough erupted from Agnes's room. Ignoring the drama queen upstairs, Deirdre grabbed her massage bag and with an "I'll be back in a while" shut the front door and followed Heather and Derek to the rehearsals.

She had a feeling in her intuition . . .

Derek introduced Deirdre to the cast, then explained about the script.

Poosie Nancy was their dame who up till that morning was the ex rugby playing ex sports teacher. A barrel-like elderly man who, built like a short round bear, had only to don an apron to get a laugh. Once he heard Mr George "Pumpernickel" was no longer directing he jumped at the chance to be in the panto. After one phone call, he was off his stationary bike and out onto his drive heading for the first script meeting. But thanks to a swift skid on an iced drive he was now being prepped "as we speak" for a hip op.

Derek sighed. "Without Poosie the deck chair scene is a farce. I was hoping that with the fairy godmother we could have made adjustments . . ."

Deirdre nodded as Little Red Riding Hood handed her a milky tea.

"The pole dancing is your ace card," said the postman, nodding to Lucinda onstage taking instructions from the choreographer.

"And the salsa dancers," muttered the choreographer, who also happened to be the salsa teacher.

"Yes, but without Poosie Nancy, the comic effect is . . . lost."

"Who's thinking of comedy with pole dancing?" said a voice from the back.

"Or salsa dancing," muttered the choreographer.

"The point is," said Derek, "we are short of a Poosie Nancy and now a fairy godmother."

Deirdre sipped her tea as the other cast members shuffled their scripts.

"Guess we were a bit hard on her," said Red Riding Hood, passing around a plate of custard creams. "I mean the auditioning, we should have checked."

"That was George," said Heather.

"And the teapot costume, must have hurt," muttered the voice from the back.

"Guess we could have been more supportive," muttered another.

"Supportive?" said the postman. "That woman has an ego the size of a whale." He looked at Deirdre. "That's what Lesley says."

"Lesley?" said Deirdre. "When were you speaking to her?"

"The other day, she's staying at the hotel," said the postman.

"Lesley's here?" said Deirdre.

The postman nodded.

Derek looked into Deirdre's sweet face. "Can't you persuade Agnes?"

Deirdre's heart skipped a beat. She looked onto the stage, catching Lucinda mid cartwheel; her intuition struck.

"Tell me about Poosie," she said, and before long she knew what to do.

Lesley didn't stay in Glasgow long. She spent one night at a friend's house and after visiting three gay bars knew she was in the wrong place. Bald men dressed in tight jeans and white T-shirts, women with short back and sides looking more like men than, well, the men. It was not her scene.

One woman pulled her to her feet and before she knew it she had her pelvis crushed against the young woman's velvet trousers. She was young enough to be her granddaughter.

"You look like you've been around a bit," she whispered, then offered her a spliff.

The last time Lesley had been offered one of those was when she was in the midst of a bra-burning festival in pre-Agnes days. Even in those days she had never been on the prowl. To be honest, all that "pulling" scared her.

She went back to the hotel in Inveraray, where she helped out and asked for a staff room. Before long she was filling in for all the staff she annoyed, upset, and offended in the kitchen. Lesley without Agnes was like a bear with a sore tooth.

And feeling lonely didn't help.

Deirdre met the hotel manager. She, like many, had heard about the "crabbit cook." The manager, sceptical about Deirdre's plans, took a bit of convincing, but Deirdre was desperate. Her hands armed with the right oils could "tame a lion," she told him, and she almost convinced herself.

The manager walked into the kitchen. Lesley, in the midst of stuffing a small bird into a larger bird, looked up. She had spent the morning growling at the kitchen porter.

The manager sighed. She had managed to make one chef sick and another leave; something had to be done, but a massage?

"There is a new massager applying to work in the spa," said the manager.

"Spa? Didn't know we had one," said Lesley.

"We don't, but we are thinking of it; apparently, it's a money spinner."

Lesley tutted.

"And we want you to give her the once-over."

"Me?" Lesley looked up, her hands covered in stuffing.

"Yes you."

"I hate that sort of thing," said Lesley.

"Exactly," he muttered.

10

THE MASSAGE

The powers of persuasion sometimes need a little oiling.

*D*eirdre stared at her oils wondering if geranium and basil would make a good mix. She had taken a selection of her best candles, several thick towels, her deluxe heated massage table and prepared the room for Lesley.

Come hell or high water this was going to work.

She watched from behind the curtain as Lesley entered the massage room . . . Deirdre looked at Lesley's rigid, short back and sides and the slop of her shoulders and realised behind that tough exterior was a woman who hadn't laughed in a long time and needed to.

Lesley made herself comfortable on the table, the warm shag pile towel enveloped her flesh, she breathed in the basil aroma and coughed.

This had better be good.

Deirdre's soft footsteps entered, she pulled the towel from Lesley's large expansive back, placed a warm firm hand on the bottom of her spine and, with a gulp grounded herself.

It was now or never.

Deirdre knew Lesley was a woman with a taut muscular back; she had seen her in action in the garden. She looked down at Lesley's muscles, tense underneath the pads of flesh. It was, as she suspected, a back that ached.

Where to start?

She went with her intuition and touched the right shoulder blade.

Lesley grimaced.

"Your shoulders are stiff," said Deirdre.

"It's sleeping on a couch that does it," said Lesley.

Deirdre with a firm grasp found a knot and dug deep.

"Owww . . ."

She dug deeper.

"Jesus . . ."

She moved with a circular motion picking up tension and tight muscles working deep into the tissue. Then she trailed her hands down the lower back, picking up more knots of tension.

"Not so hard."

Deirdre carried on making her way near the kidneys.

Lesley screamed.

Then as Deirdre released with a soothing rub, Lesley's body flopped with release.

"What are you trying to do, kill me?"

Deirdre with a brisk flick of the towel revealed Lesley's thighs she moved to the upper inside leg.

"Careful that's my . . . owww . . . tender bit . . ."

"It's very knotted," muttered Deirdre

"Yes but . . . ouch . . . blimey . . . shit . . . that hurts . . . ooooh . . . oooh . . . oh . . ."

Deirdre released another tough muscle. "You have dancer thighs," she muttered.

"Aye right."

"Seriously, dancing is the only thing that is going to release your problem."

"What problem?"

"You have back pain, right?"

"Who hasn't."

"Joint ache?"

"No."

"Well you will soon."

Lesley jolted. "What?"

"And pelvic tension, do you have any?" said Deirdre.

Lesley turned her head. "What is this, the third degree?"

Deirdre manipulated her head back into place. Lesley heard a familiar grunt. She knew that grunt anywhere.

"Wait a minute, I know you."

"And laughter would do wonders for these muscles," muttered Deirdre. "A few more sessions and you'll be a new woman—flying."

"You're the kitchen porter, aren't you?"

Deirdre lifted her oil bottle and began to pour more oil onto her hands.

"Know your greasy paws anywhere . . ." said Lesley.

The bottle of basil oil slipped from Deirdre's hand and before it landed on the floor, Lesley stuck her hand out and caught it. Then she turned to see Deirdre.

"Miss Muffet?"

Quaking inside, Deirdre matched her stare. "Another rub?"

"From you? Don't think so, rather have pins stuck in my eyes," said Lesley.

"Acupuncture then?"

"What?" said Lesley.

"Healing with pins. Great for back pain," said Deirdre.

Lesley glared. "Aye, right."

"Agnes hates the idea, but then she is a bit of a coward," rambled Deirdre.

Lesley eyed her nemesis. "What you up to?"

"Agnes's fear of pain has totally blocked her healing, but I see you are different. Don't you feel better?"

Lesley repositioned herself on the table for a better view of Miss Muffet. *There's more to this tiny tot than first thought.*

Deirdre tentatively massaged Lesley's shoulder; it felt so good.

"She's a fairy godmother now," said Deirdre.

"Her in a tutu and wings?"

"Yes, it's a comic part; she's to play an ex-chocoholic who can't remember names, let alone spells."

"As if."

"No leggings," said Deirdre.

"My heart bleeds for her."

"No high boots."

"Poor soul."

"But apparently the best gig in the panto, and the most laughs."

"As if I care," said Lesley.

Deirdre moved down her arm, rubbing in the warm oil. "In fact, the only part better than that is the dame, Poosie Nancy."

Lesley tutted as Deirdre rubbed some oil into Lesley's right hand. "Is there pain here too?"

"Oooh."

"Yes, Poosie Nancy is the real star, steals all the laughs from the fairy godmother . . . especially the deck chair scene," said Deirdre.

She eased Lesley back into the prone position and began to manipulate her neck.

"Poosie truly gets to rain on the fairy godmother's parade," muttered Deirdre.

Lesley closed her eyes. "Shut up and keep rubbing."

Deirdre continued to massage Lesley's head and face. She loosened the muscles around her neck, all the while chatting about Poosie. Lesley almost fell asleep, and by the time Deirdre had finished, Lesley's round face was shiny, smooth, and relaxed. She left the treatment room walking like a dancer as Deirdre began to whistle.

"Beware of a woman who whistles," chuckled a cleaner. "It usually means she's making plans."

Lesley stopped. She felt happy, a first in a long time.

Two more massages and Lesley was ripe for the picking. With her back sorted, her pelvis supple, and her bloating gone, Lesley felt like a new woman. Suddenly, dancing with deck chairs sounded like a hoot and definitely better than spending a night on the couch undoing all Deirdre's good work.

And as for the thought of annoying Agnes, not to mention meeting pole dancing Lucinda, watching *Strictly* seemed positively boring.

Now all Deirdre had to do was convince Agnes . . .

In the end, all it took was one picture in the local paper and an "A Star Is Born" article to rile Agnes into action.

Derek and Deirdre stayed up all night working on the article. Over coffee and cake they came up with a piece that annoyed even a comatose "high on Night Nurse" Agnes.

As Agnes lingered over her early morning coffee toying with the idea of going back to bed, Deirdre poked the middle page spread under her nose.

There in her silver hot pants, mid mop, was a bright-looking Lucinda winking at the camera. Agnes, coffee suspended, read the article . . .

No more mops for our favourite singer . . .

She's off to cartwheel happiness at the old folks' home. And you can catch her live at the Little Red Riding Hood panto. A woman who dances, sings, and tells stories, not only on stage but up a pole.

"She's our best principal boy ever," says Derek the director, and there's no stopping her.

She already has bookings from Aberdeen to Arran.

Agnes choked on her coffee. "A principal on a pole . . . stealing the show?"

She tossed her crust at the cat. "How dare they . . ."

Then she stopped, looked, right at the bottom of the article . . .

"I can't wait to work with her," says Lesley, our local chef. "It's my first pantomime and stepping into Poosie Nancy's shoes is going to be a hoot."

"Hoot . . . since when did that turncoat say hoot?"

The cat mid lick of her crust was quickly shooed with a fluffy slipper. Agnes was livid. Tossing the paper across the room, she rose from her seat as her morose grief turned to the fiery "I'll show her" of a woman scorned.

"Get me my lucky leggings," shouted Agnes. "I've a rehearsal tonight."

11

MRS MCCRACKIN & THE CO-OP

A seatbelt is not always necessary.

*B*eing in Derek's panto was a whole new experience for the cast. Derek had never been anything but a flop on stage and an embarrassment to the panto. Offstage, however, he seemed to know what worked, and he and Charlie the writer worked well together. Standing up to his mother changed him; shaking free of his mother's grip and her dream to make into a younger version of his father emancipated Derek. And Charlie understood, they had the same vision and the same sense of humour.

Agnes never did comedy; she was strictly a "get a load of her" sort of actress who in her time had received wolf whistles on and off stage. Not now, Agnes could not remember the last wolf whistle she had heard. It was, to quote Heather, "time for a change" . . . perhaps now she should aim for laughs.

On the day of the first rehearsal, Deidre woke up and walked to the kitchen, and for the first time ever the tea cupboard was free to open. Deirdre flicked the kettle on, opened the cupboard, and spent a leisurely few minutes surveying the selection.

Bliss . . .

Agnes was still in her room. She had spent the morning preparing for her first rehearsal. She had her lucky leggings laid out on the spare bed, her makeup standing to attention by her mirror, and her script read at least three times and underlined.

She looked at herself in the mirror . . .

No more thigh-high boots and whips for her. Now she had a wand that didn't work, a spell book with pages missing, and a Little Red Riding Hood who answered back. She was the hapless fairy godmother with a chocolate addiction, a drink problem, a poor memory for names, and, damn it, the funniest character in the show. She would make sure of that.

Deirdre sipped her first stress-free morning herbal with an "arrrh." No Agnes, no Lesley, and no hacking cough from above . . .

Perhaps she had time for another?

Agnes brushed her hair, pulled a face, and then spied Lesley's empty closet behind her in the mirror.

How dare she, after all she put me through? It was her job to admire, pamper, and encourage, not steal the limelight.

She opened the closet, then shut it again; a thought hit her . . .

She went into Deirdre's room, stood in front of the deer head, and pulled away the yin-yang flag that covered it. The glass-eyed apparition stared back.

She wondered how heavy it was.

"This deer head," shouted Agnes, "do you think it will fit in the car?"

Deirdre, mid third "arrrh," looked up.

"What was that?"

And then without waiting for an answer she gulped her tea and went upstairs.

When Lesley arrived at her first rehearsal, her stomach jumped with anticipation. She had the strut of a happy pelvis, a windless stomach, and the back of a woman with aligned core muscles. She could not wait to meet Agnes and show her who could really steal the show.

Then, the icing on the cake . . . watching and, yes, meeting a real live pole dancer.

Deirdre arrived at the rehearsal with Agnes. Derek motioned to the seat next to him; she smiled as Agnes appeared behind her clutching the deer head.

The cast, in hushed silence, stared.

Derek pulled a "what the hell is that" face.

"Don't ask," said Deirdre.

She had spent twenty minutes manoeuvring the deer head into the back seat of the car. Agnes, ignoring Deirdre's "I could use a hand," eyed herself in the rear vision mirror and hummed. Realising that a seat belt was not enough, Deirdre spent a further twenty minutes manipulating a belt along with said seat belt to hold it in place. Then with an "are you satisfied?" she squeezed herself into the front seat, avoiding any eye poking of antlers. Agnes, still looking at the rear vision mirror, caught sight of the two glass eyes. She stopped humming. "How did you sleep at night?"

Deirdre huffed. "It was a nightmare getting here," she said to Derek.

"I thought you said don't ask."

"And that Mrs McCrackin didn't help."

Derek sagely nodded.

Mrs McCrackin, an elderly woman with a bad sense of timing, was driving down the street in a race to catch the co-op before it shut. Ignoring the traffic lights, she swerved across the road. Agnes's emergency stop torpedoed the deer head into the top of the front seat, skewing Deirdre's ponytail, which took another twenty minutes for Mrs McCrackin and Agnes to untangle.

"I would have been quicker doing it myself," said Deirdre, "but try telling a deaf eighty-year-old and a humming, no, *singing* Agnes to stop?"

She gestured to the postman up a ladder, drill posed. "May as well try and get ol' postie up there to stop telling every man and his dog about pole-dancing Lucinda."

Derek looked at Deirdre's interestingly ruffled hair and wanted to tell her she looked beautiful. Instead he laughed, muttering, "I can just imagine."

Agnes marched up to the stage and dumped the deer head onto it. "For the forest scene," she said, looking about for Lesley.

Lesley appeared from the side, mid corset tying, and threw Agnes a blank-faced stare. . .

The cast watched as she meandered around the head, noting any marks or dents, then looked at Agnes. "Great idea."

Agnes stunned, silently watching as Lesley, relishing her moment, waltzed back to the side of the stage.

Lesley one, me nil, thought Agnes, taking a seat at the back of the hall.

12

THE CHASE SCENE

Not all attention is wanted.

*D*uring the first act rehearsals, Lesley and Agnes were not onstage together, but that did not stop them watching each other and making notes. Each wanted to be the best, most comical, and they embraced their roles with a grim determination that at times smacked of desperation.

Lesley joined the gym, building up her muscles for a more masculine-looking Poosie Nancy. While Agnes, getting into the swing of her fairy godmother part, began to practise whispery voices, working on her scatterbrain characterisation.

However, neither could compete with the four new salsa dancers who, for some reason, wore tap dancing shoes. Their cute factor was huge, being that they were all of primary school age. For them, getting a laugh required a mere skid or a mispronounced "Poosie." In fact, they loved the reaction so much they said "Pussy" every chance they could —with or without the dancing.

Agnes and Lesley had to work hard to grab the limelight and, apart from holding up the rehearsals, few of their attempts worked. How could a middle-aged woman get a laugh when most of her scenes involved a principal boy cartwheeling in hot pants tighter than cling film?

How could a middle-aged woman with a few lines about a soup kitchen compete with four girls tap dancing to salsa songs and shouting "Pussy" whenever they had the chance? Especially when one had a lisp?

A month into the rehearsals and the cast, still stuck on the first act, were at a breaking point. Agnes reworked every direction, gag, and song as the cast members lined up waiting for their queue. And Lesley had taken to ad-libbing . . .

"That so-called fairy godmother . . . been at the chocolate again—so she says."

"That so-called fairy godmother . . . been at the cooking sherry again—cooking—so she says."

Finally, as Agnes stood in front of Granny's Soup Kitchen tap dancing and telling an unscripted joke, the postman, posed by his lighting equipment, lost it. For a month he had waited for the pole dancing scene and the only pole he had seen was the wicked wolf's walking stick.

"Can we not just stick to the script," he yelled.

Agnes sheepishly stopped. "But my tap dancing's funny."

"As funny as a knock-knock joke?" muttered the postman.

The salsa team lined up at the side of the stage, giggling. Fed up waiting, they had been "mucking about," catcalling, "here pussy, pussy, pussy," and Lesley's agitation was, like the postman's, at boiling point. She had spent the last hour crammed into her costume while Deloris marked adjustments about her muscular torso. And she was a pin's prick away from losing it.

"Shall we move on?" said Derek. He looked about. "Where's Poosie?"

"Here pussy, pussy, pussy . . ."

"It's Poosie Nancy," snapped Lesley, retrieving a pin from her armpit.

"Puthy . . ."

A giggle erupted.

"One more pussy . . ." snapped Lesley with a toss of her pin. "Just one more . . . I dare you."

"Shall we move on to the next scene?" said Derek. He looked about the hall. "Lucinda?"

Silence . . .

"Where's Lucinda?" said Derek.

"She's gone for the messages," said a voice from the back.

"Messages?" said Derek.

"She's gone home," said another.

"Fed up waiting like the rest of us," muttered the postman.

"She's gone to feed the pussy," said a small voice, followed by stifled giggles.

"Right, that is it, you twerps are for it," snapped Lesley.

"Twerps?" muttered one.

"I am here," shouted Lucinda.

The cast stopped and stared at Lucinda, posed like a caped crusader in her principal boy outfit.

She strutted up to the stage, looked at the salsa girls. "Isn't it past your bedtime?" Then she eyed Lesley. "Nice costume, Poosie Nancy."

Rehearsal for the second half was shorter and much sweeter, as most of the lines for the fairy godmother had been cut.

Lesley, watching the line cutting off her ex-partner, toned down her ad-libbing antics.

Instead she watched old Charlie Chaplin and Laurel and Hardy films and learnt to react with her face and gestures. She watched reruns of pantomime on YouTube and comedians dressed as women; the Two Ronnie's, Stanley Baxter, and Les Dawson. Soon she had mastered the under-the-breast cross-arm favoured by Les Dawson, Stanley Baxter's impersonation of the queen, and Ronnie Barker's Dolly Parton.

Lucinda was so impressed she offered to give her a few pole dancing lessons, and when the salsa dancers wanted to join in, she agreed as long as they stopped the "pussy" catcalling.

Lesley was smitten.

After every rehearsal, she threw her muscular gym body up the pole and found a passion for movement she had never felt before. Despite her large, muscular frame, she was graceful and light on her feet, and Derek was so impressed he wrote it into the show.

Lucinda and Lesley practised pole dancing after the rehearsals. Lesley's torso firmed up, her army pants became looser, and Agnes's pain increased. She lingered, watching in the dark as Lesley and Lucinda laughed, joked, and even at times hugged after Lesley accomplished a new move.

She lingered until tears welled up.

An unbearable emptiness engulfed Agnes, a pain in her heart she'd never felt before, and the only thing that made it go away was gin and cookery programs on TV.

It was only when they got to the deck chair scene near the end of the second act that Agnes and Lesley had to work together. A chase scene Derek had come to dread as much as the postman yearned for.

The scene was set in front of Poosie Nancy's soup kitchen . . .

While the fairy godmother sleeps in a deck chair accompanied by "over the top" snoring, Poosie Nancy rustles up a giant-sized milkshake in a milk bucket, to fit her "gob."

Both are taken by surprise when the wolf disguised as an elderly grandpa grabs the milkshake with his cane.

The fairy godmother jumps, shouts, and chases, followed by the salsa girls (appearing from nowhere) and Poosie Nancy. The chase runs through the audience and back onto the stage where the wolf disappears up a magic beanstalk with a demonic "Ha-ha-ha," followed by Lucinda (also appearing from nowhere).

There is a flash, a bang, and a cardboard cutout wolf falls from the ceiling along with his walking stick; the beanstalk facade drops to reveal a pole.

Lucinda, having "caught the wolf," pole dances down the pole, accompanied by the salsa girls, singing "Ding-Dong, the Wolf Is Dead."

The scene ends with Poosie Nancy and the fairy godmother both grabbing the milkshake bucket, leading to a tossing of the bucket (full of confetti) into the audience. An old panto trick which Charlie feared could lead to Agnes over-egging the whole scene, to a point that she may not leave the stage ever again. Which Charlie pointed out was a total exaggeration, not to mention impossible.

"Is the dame ready?" shouted Derek.

"Just a minute," shouted Deloris.

"I'm ready," squeaked Agnes with her best whimsical voice.

"What?" shouted Derek.

"She says she's ready," shouted the postman, rolling out his extra-long cable.

"Who?"

"The fairy godmother."

Charlie sighed.

The cast walked through the scene.

Lucinda slid down the pole; the salsa girls moved backstage, preparing for their chorus, as Agnes loitered.

"Off the stage, Agnes," said Derek.

"Just preparing for the bucket scene."

Derek turned to Charlie. "Knew this would happen. Do you think we should scrap the scene?"

"What, the pole dance? We'll have a mutiny."

"I am talking about Agnes and her bucket," said Derek.

Charlie looked at the postman, posed by his lighting equipment. "We could throw in some strobe lighting."

"During a pole dance? Lucinda will go mental," said Derek.

"Strobe lighting for the bucket scene," said Charlie.

Could work. Could contain the scene, thought Derek.

"And use the wind machine for the pole dancing," said Charlie.

"Wind machine on Lucinda?" Derek's face lit up. "That'll keep the postman happy and Herself offstage."

13

THE POLE

A performance without stage fright is not a performance but a walk in the park.

The dress rehearsal was held at the Heavenly Space retirement village. The special effects were kept to a minimum and the strobe light banned.

It took an hour to seat the audience, and by the time all were seated, the first to arrive were dozing.

Derek, who had arranged for Deirdre to "shoulder massage" some of the cast, sent her out into the audience to give "wake-up hand massages where required."

"I am in the middle of sorting the narrator's panic attack," whispered Deirdre.

"Agnes can deal with that, she's not on for a while."

Agnes, resembling a drag queen in her pancake makeup, looked up from her mirror. "Me, massage? Wouldn't know where to start."

"Just wave the oils under her nose and tell her to breathe," muttered Deirdre with a glare at Derek.

"Breathe?" said Agnes. "Isn't that a bit obvious?"

The narrator, with a face like a startled chicken, looked at Agnes. "It's no good, I can't go on."

Snatching the oil bottle from Deirdre, Agnes waved it under the narrator's nose.

"Breathe."

The narrator inhaled, then coughed.

"It's OK," said Agnes with a robust pat on the back.

The narrator spluttered. "OK? My nana's out there, front row, and she's got a voice like a lion's roar."

"She's asleep."

"Aye, but for how long? Once the salsa's started she'll be awake, poised for a good shout."

Agnes tutted. "But that's what panto is all about, shouting—the audience love it."

"I know, that's what I am afraid of."

Agnes had seen the startled chicken look before. She softened her voice. "You'll be fine."

"Easy for you to say."

Agnes gestured to the audience. "Look out there. What do you see?"

The narrator stared out onto a sea of faces half asleep. A carer lifted a cup of tea from a dozing gentleman, Deirdre rubbed the hand of a women singing "It's a Long Way to Tipperary." And right at the front row on her nana's knee sat the resident fat black cat, his claws needling her chest as she dozed.

"It's the perfect first audience—they're half asleep, even their tea is going cold. If you make a mistake, who's going to notice?"

"Hmmm."

"Half of them can't even hear."

The narrator's face softened. "Suppose so."

"And they don't know the script."

"That's true."

"If you make a mistake, who will know?"

"I guess . . . no one." The narrator almost smiled.

"That's my girl," said Agnes. "Now, when you walk on, count your breath."

"Count my breath?"

"It relaxes you."

"Relax, what about my lines—I'll forget." The narrator began to panic again.

"But you've got the narrator book, just slip the script in like this . . ."

"Jesus, forgot about that."

"Look at me, I used to be just like you."

"Really?"

"Puked my guts many a time before a performance."

"There's no need to be so graphic."

"Now, walking on stage is like peeling a banana," lied Agnes.

"Peeling a banana?" muttered the narrator with a confused look. Agnes nudged the narrator out onto the stage . . .

"Shhh, here's the nurse," said one of the carers.

"What?" yelled a deaf gentleman.

The narrator's nana woke up. "Nurse?" she barked.

The narrator looked at Agnes.

Agnes mimed peeling a banana with a "go on" look.

"Is that the dame?" shouted another.

"That's my Gillie?" said the narrator's nana.

"Isn't she gay?" said a voice from the back.

"Gay?" The narrator's gran stood and looked around. "She's a nurse."

"Sit down," yelled an older man at the back.

"She's got three kids," she huffed.

"It doesn't matter who's gay," said the carer, redirecting the grandma to a sitting position.

"It's the dame that's gay," huffed the narrator's nana.

"The dame's a man, always a man," muttered a voice from the back.

"Once upon a time," started the narrator . . .

After the dress rehearsal, Agnes decided not to hang around for the coffee and chat . . .

The narrator had completely forgotten Agnes and her pep talk. After her first laugh, she, smitten with the attention, began to bound onto the stage like a pro, finally receiving a standing ovation for her narration of the chase scene, which she performed in a clipped South African auctioneer voice.

Never before had her nana looked so proud.

Nana had spent most of her life in South Africa and hardly knew "her Gillie," except that she was an OK nurse who could do with a larger uniform, spent most of her visits flirting with any man who looked her way, and had three children she'd rather not see.

Nana had no idea her Gillie had it in her . . . to entertain. She watched her Gillie tuck into her third bite-sized quiche and for the first time said nothing about her waistline. Instead she poured her a dram and introduced her to all who walked past. The old boy who had been sitting next to Nana, star-struck and deaf, shouted like a referee on a field.

"You were great," he yelled.

"He said you were great," barked Nana.

"I heard," said the narrator.

"You could do that for a living," he shouted.

"He said you should give up nursing . . ." barked Nana.

"I heard," said the narrator.

"She's thinking about it," said Nana.

"Have another quiche, Nana."

Lucinda's pole dancing was also a hit, surrounded by a couple of carers and few residents she along with Lesley worked a few moves.

One frail woman inspired by her half a pint of stout wrapped her bony leg around the pole and inched herself off the ground.

The carers sprung to attention.

"Easy."

"Mind."

"Let's get down, shall we?"

"How about some quiche?"

Lucinda laughed. "She's an ex-fireman, she knows all about poles, don't you love?" And gave her a round of applause.

Agnes watched with a dark feeling. *Did she have to be so frigging nice?*

The frail woman's small face beamed like a full moon. And Lesley, looking totally at home and serine, gave her a gentle "good on you love" pat.

Agnes sipped her milky tea. *What had happened to Lesley?*

The Lesley she knew oiled mowers, trimmed hedges, chopped

wood, all with the whistle of a plumber happy at his work. What was she doing prancing about a pole, let alone being congenial with the elderly?

Her Lesley was as congenial as a gas bill, a real loner, and that was what she loved about *her* Lesley.

Agnes sighed. Who was going to keep the outside tidy now? Who was she going to soothe and manage? She felt like a used tissue, as out of date as her knock-knock jokes.

She grabbed her jacket and looked back; Lucinda was now giving the carers a shot at the pole. She had heard about their plans to teach pole dancing, an idea embraced by all in the cast, including the salsa teacher.

"Come join us," said Lucinda, to Nana.

Agnes could not take any more. She sloped home, poured herself a gin—skipping the lemon and ice, or "the frilly bits," as Lesley used to call it—and plonked herself in front of *Celebrity Chef*.

14

GIN, TV, AND A CAT

A cat by any other name still needs to be fed.

By the time Deirdre arrived home, Agnes had polished off a jumbo pack of crisps, slipped into Lesley's sweat pants, and was glaring at Jamie Oliver with a "no one wants me" slump.

She looked a sad sight.

"I have a new life now," she muttered.

Deirdre spied the half-empty gin bottle.

"Gin . . ." She gestured with her glass. ". . . the TV." She looked down at the cat on her knee. "And a cat to throw things at . . ."

"Well that's nothing to crow about," muttered Deirdre.

Agnes thumped her hand on the cat's head. ". . . and pat."

The cat with no name grimaced.

"And you know what," she slurred, "I might just give this cat a name . . . chop my own bleeding wood, even . . ." She took a large sip. "Get a frigging gardener!"

Deirdre sighed; she thought Lesley and Agnes would be together by now and she would be in a new flat. Instead, Agnes had stopped eating and swilled gin like tea. Deirdre had cooked Agnes's favourite food and tried to convince Agnes that there was life after Lesley and leggings. And when that didn't work, she pulled out photos of the past, attempting to ignite happy memories along with a "you still have plenty more to make" lecture.

Agnes waved the photos away with the TV remote.

Deirdre had no idea what to do next apart from leaving her to it . . . but how could she? Agnes had helped her, taken her in, told everyone about her creams. The Vegan Is the New Black shop was now in the black thanks to Agnes, and despite her "I want to be alone" mantra, Deirdre knew she shouldn't be and definitely didn't mean it.

Derek, arriving after Deirdre and catching the words "gardener" and "wood," looked quizzically at Deirdre.

Derek had taken to driving Deirdre home in the vain hope that he would find the courage to ask her out. He nudged Deirdre and pointed to the gin bottle.

"Did you not have any tea?" said Deirdre.

"They are going to run pole dancing classes," muttered Agnes. "Together."

"It's just a class," muttered Deirdre.

"You could join," said Derek.

Agnes didn't react but with a sniff drained her glass, flicked off the TV, and, hitching up the oversized sweat pants, made for her bed. "That is the last place I would want to be."

Deirdre and Derek watched Agnes climb the stairs like it was Mount Everest, every step an effort.

"Can't wait for it all to be over," she muttered. "Then I'll never have to face that Lucinda and her frigging pole ever . . ."—a few steps—". . . ever . . ."—at the landing—". . . again . . ."

"She used to love being onstage," muttered Derek.

"I know."

"So sure of herself. Can't believe it."

"She even refused a massage," muttered Deirdre.

Lucinda cartwheeled off the stage, wowing the audience. It was the last night and the hall was full of families and friends of the cast.

Agnes stood under the heat of the stage lights waiting for her cue. She was to be in the deck chair, snoring like a walrus, when the curtains opened. Agnes looked out onto the stage; what she wouldn't do for gin and a cat to metaphorically kick.

The curtains were closed, and the narrator was in front pushing the story forward with jokes and a song. While the postman (on tippy-toes) and Heather (whispering that there was no need for tippy-toes) moved the scenery into place for the chase scene.

Derek had gone all out with props. As the postman surveyed the scene, he wondered if perhaps a little too much . . . wind machine and a strobe light. *What was he, a magician two places at the one time?*

The first night he raced from the strobe light to the wind machine and missed half the pole dance. Lucinda, a vision of loveliness, told him it didn't matter, he was only human. But the "only human" had missed most of the pole dance, which to him was not only the icing on the cake but the cherry on top of the icing on the cake.

She was lovely.

The second night he set up a timer on the wind machine; it started halfway through the chase scene, clearing the stage of half the deck chairs. Luckily, the audience thought it was all part of the act, and for a moment Derek wondered if it was possible to recreate until the postman threw him a look . . .

The third night the timing was perfect but, thanks to an overzealous moving of props behind stage, the aim of the wind machine was a little off. It blew into the audience, scattering crisp packets across the stage like tumbleweed in a desert. The wolf slipped on one mid chase and nearly blew the timing of the scene.

Tonight was the postman's last night . . . he cemented the wind machine in position with a mountain of sandbags and hissed at any who walked near it.

The postman took his position by the strobe light, Heather on a beam posed by the top of the calico beanstalk over the pole.

The trap door was unlocked.

The deck chairs arranged.

The wind machine timer checked—aim perfect.

The strobe light warmed up and switched to pause . . .

"All clear," whispered the postman into his head mic.

"OK, stand by," muttered Derek. He cued the cast.

Agnes took her place.

The curtains opened and Agnes, eyes closed, let out a loud snore in the deck chair.

The audience chuckled.

Lesley in full Poosie Nancy mode hummed behind the Granny's Soup Kitchen facade.

She peeked through the serving hatch waving the milk bucket. "This'll keep the ol' goat happy."

She winked at the audience. "Shall I?"

"Yes!" shouted the audience.

Lesley placed the bucket by Agnes.

Agnes let out another humungous snore as her hand flopped by the side of the deck chair into the bucket.

She jumped. "Oh, Lordy Lord!"

The audience laughed . . .

The chase scene started; the strobe light flicked on . . .

Perfect, thought Derek.

So far so good, thought the postman.

Heather looked at her watch, regretting the lack of decent dinner; her stomach rumbled.

The salsa dancer chased the wolf around the audience, then up onto the stage. The wolf headed up the bean pole. The salsa girls exited for a quick change into their "Ding-Dong the Wolf Is Dead" number.

Heather on cue pulled the lever to drop the bean stalk facade . . . it stuck like an out-of-date jam jar . . .

Lucinda waited . . .

Derek, seeing the "what the bollocks?" look on Heather's face, shouted into his head mic, "Give it a good tug."

There was a clang from the ceiling, followed by a trail of hissed swear words.

Charlie by the side of the stage, script in hand ready to prompt, looked up.

"Shit," hissed the postman by the strobe lights. He raced to Heather, stumbling into the "This way to Granny's Soup Kitchen" sign in a so-called "walkway" space. His ingrown toenail throbbed . . .

"Shit!"

Lesley looked at Agnes with a "what do we do" look.

Silence . . .

Agnes grasped the scene in an instant. She'd been here before: lines forgotten, props missing. She was unfazed, she was a pro.

Her actor's mind raced. She had a set of wings, a wand, and a layer of petticoats on par with an onion, and she knew the wind machine was about to start.

She knew what to do.

15

THE WIND MACHINE

Laughter speaks louder than words.

Agnes moved into position . . .

The wind machine on cue started, billowing her dress, ruffling her petticoat high above her head. She pulled the infamous Marilyn Monroe white dress pose, which in her fairy godmother outfit got a laugh.

She followed with a Marilyn Monroe pout.

More laughs . . .

"Good heavens," she shouted, "you got some view of my knickers."

The audience continued to laugh.

Agnes waved her wand as she swirled; her wings caught in her petticoat.

"Keep going," whispered Charlie.

Agnes flashed a look at Heather—Heather pulled a "still no pole" look.

Agnes motioned to Lesley to walk behind the soup kitchen.

"We better shake a leg," she shouted.

Lesley looked puzzled.

"A storm is a-brewing."

Lesley with a questioning look at her ex moved behind the

Granny's Soup Kitchen screen as Agnes, her instincts on fire, mimed walking against a blizzard with an out-of-control petticoat.

Laughter filled the hall.

"The ol' pro," muttered Derek.

"Magic," whispered Charlie.

Almost offstage, Agnes stopped, turned, Lesley now behind the screen . . .

"Where's that Poosie?"

The audience laughed. "Behind the kitchen!"

Agnes put a hand to her ear. "What?"

"Behind you."

"Here, pussy, pussy . . ."

"It's Poosie Nancy!" shouted Lesley.

The children giggle.

Agnes pointed to the kitchen. "Here?"

Children squeal with delight.

Agnes walked behind the kitchen and pushed Lesley out in front.

By the time Lucinda was swinging on her pole, the audience were laughing so hard they were crying. Lesley and Agnes had milked the audience with an old Laurel and Hardy routine which had the audiences in stitches. Lesley followed Agnes; she understood her nods, looks, and gestures, and within seconds they were synced as only thirty years of living together could do.

As Agnes went behind the soup kitchen, Lesley searched in front, as she went behind, Agnes came out looking for her. Agnes puffed with pleasure; she had no idea that getting a laugh could feel so good.

At the end of the show, as the performers lined up for their bow, Lucinda and the narrator pushed Lesley to the back and turned to Agnes.

"You're on last with Lesley," said Lucinda. "You saved the show."

Each character walked out for their bow: the wolf, the salsa dancer, Lucinda, and Red Riding Hood.

Under the hot lights, Agnes and Lesley stood together waiting to take their bow.

Agnes turned to Lesley. "One more time?"

The curtains opened; the audience cheered.

Lesley took her arm and they walked onto the stage.

Agnes bowed to a standing applause, and as the postman flicked the wind machine on she pulled her final Marilyn Monroe pose for the season.

That night, Agnes went home a changed woman. She always saw herself as a blonde bombshell with a pair of legs demanding attention. Tonight, dressed as a drag queen, she made them laugh, and she did it with Lesley.

She basked in the praise of the cast, she lingered at the aftershow party, and when Lucinda joked with Lesley, Agnes for once was too busy chatting to the narrator to notice.

The narrator lived several miles away and was looking for a lift. Agnes, being in a generous mood, was happy to not only give her a lift but relive the magic moment of applause.

Agnes packed her things into a case as family and friends helped with the tidying up of the hall. She didn't notice the young man with a drill at the bottom of the pole.

"Great news about Lucinda," said the narrator.

Agnes tutted.

"She's getting married."

Agnes stopped. "They're getting married?" Her Lesley.

Agnes looked across at Lesley lifting the pole onto the ground. She said something, and the young man laughed.

"Bit sudden, they hardly know each other."

The narrator gestured to the young man now dismantling the pole, while Lesley packed sections into it case.

"They have known each other for years."

"Years?"

"He's a pole dancer too."

"He?"

"Yes, look at him, the body of an athlete. They are going to use him in the next panto."

Agnes stared at the young man, who had moved on to detaching parts of the scenery.

All that angst and gin, thought Agnes, *and there was Lucinda with a man all along.*

"Two pole dancers," she muttered. "In *Cinderella?*"

"I know," said the narrator. "What a hoot."

A week after the panto and Agnes was standing in the kitchen. She had just heard that the panto players had plans for fundraising, including an auction, a raffle, a coffee morning, and a spring sketch show. And Lesley was not only "up for the spring sketch" but would be glad to partner with Agnes.

Agnes looked out onto her garden. There would be script meetings, rehearsals, *and* baking: a whole new world opened to her and a whole new Agnes.

She was beginning to feel liberated from her dark cloud.

Deirdre walked in and filled the kettle.

Agnes opened the tea cupboard. "What's your poison, herbal or builder's brew?'

Deirdre looked up.

The gin hadn't been touched since the last night and Agnes was beginning to glow again. She had taken to "tidying up" outside and cooking instead of watching about it on TV. She had even looked up tablet recipes for the coffee morning and brought the ingredients.

"There is something to be said for moving on," she said.

Deirdre jiggled her tea bag.

"If you want to move on, it's OK with me." Agnes smiled.

"Thanks."

"I have things to do."

"So it seems."

"And you never know, Derek might leave his mother."

Deirdre blushed.

Six Months Later...

Agnes headed into the secondhand shop with her principal boy outfits. She was having a clear-out, making way for the redecorating of her spare room.

She handed an armful to the two women behind the counter.

"Deirdre said you'd be coming in," said a round woman. "But she didn't say the costume would be so . . ."

"Glamorous?"

"Small."

"You think they are small?" said Agnes with a coquettish smile.

"Well yeah." She held up a costume. "Wouldn't even fit one of my legs."

Agnes looked through the old wedding dresses and wondered about next year's fairy godmother; she had heard it was to be Cinderella, and Deloris had already spoken to her about ideas.

Deirdre, now living in her own flat, offered free massages as a raffle prize and gave Derek a taster. So impressed was he that he managed to sell a mountain of raffle tickets, and so relaxed and floaty was he that he didn't return to his mother's house for days.

Agnes went into the dressing room, held a dress against her, and looked into the mirror. She spied Lesley walking in, clutching the deer head like it was as light as a purse. Her stomach jumped; she hadn't seen Lesley since the panto. She thought about the final bow together arm in arm. What she'd give to be arm in arm again.

Every day, Agnes passed the secondhand shop just as she passed the hotel and Deirdre's shop. She had taken to walking more and watching TV less and often hoped in that walking that she would bump into Lesley. Every script meeting she attended she arrived excited at the thought of meeting Lesley, who was never there.

"Don't think we can sell that," said the lady.

"Why not?"

They shook their heads.

"What about the auction?"

"The manager's a vegan."

"Vegan?"

The women nodded.

Lesley stood with a hopeful "if I stand long enough, they'll change their minds" stance.

Silence.

"Bloody vegan," she muttered. And she was about to walk out when Agnes appeared from behind the curtain.

"I am doing up the spare room," said Agnes.

Lesley eyed her.

"The room is empty."

Lesley had heard that Deirdre had moved.

"You could hang it in there."

"Big job hanging this thing up." Lesley eyed her ex-partner. "It takes two."

"I know," said Agnes. "And I have some steak enough for two, and wine." Agnes smiled. "How else can I thank you?"

And Lesley, with a loud laugh, followed Agnes out to her car.

The End

Book 3 Panto Girl is out now at your favourite store.
Keep on reading for a preview

PANTO GIRL-CHAPTER ONE

The last thing Helmet was looking for was romance, the last thing Toby was looking for was a father, but Toby's mother had other ideas.

Helmut, a blogger of German origin, had just sat through a two-hour open mic session at the Stand and he hadn't laughed once. Helmut found the session as painful as a G-string two sizes too small; he was confused. He had always prided himself on his keen sense of timing and dry wit, and yet he left unmoved.

Helmut spent his time traveling while blogging about anything alternative, organic, and hopeful, and he had a good following. He had this idea for a piece on laughter therapy and decided to start with the great British dry wit.

Now he was confused . . .

Helmut walked down Great Western Road, pondering the use or abuse of the English language by its natives.

He had researched his subject before he left Germany and the Stand was *the* comedy club in Glasgow, where all the best comedians performed.

Perhaps Tuesday is not the best night to visit.

He spied a pub advertising German beer and went in. It was the same pub Lesley liked to visit, and as she was the only person sitting at the bar, he pulled up a stool beside her and offered her a drink. When she said "Maisel's Weisse," he looked at her with more interest.

Lesley had a fondness for German beer, and as they worked their way through the selection, Lesley began to open up. By the time Helmut was on his third pint, Lesley's accent became easier to understand . . .

"It was the teapot outfit that did it," said Lesley. "I told her if she was going to wear that onstage, I would not be responsible for my actions."

"Your partner is wearing a teapot?" said Helmut. "This is funny?"

"Nothing's funny about my ex," said Lesley. "Especially her principal boy."

"Principle boy?" said Helmut.

"About as camp as steak pie," she said.

"Begging your pardon?" said Helmut. "Principle boy?"

"Aye, you know, a woman dressed as a man . . . dancing . . . singing?" said Lesley.

"This is funny?" said Helmut.

"About as funny as herpes," said Lesley.

Helmut smiled. He knew about herpes.

Helmut was a young man with an earnest face and long legs that got in the way of everything. He was an ex–media student with parents who knew everything, including the great "tartan colony" of Scotland. Helmut had grown up on tales of bagpipes, football hooligans, castles, and shortbread: nothing like the Great Western Road he had just walked down. It was full of people from other countries. In fact, he was served by an Australian, got in the way of a Serbian cleaner, and managed to trip up an Indian—all in the one pub.

Lesley was the first real Scot he'd talked to, and he had lots of questions to ask. However, all she wanted to do was talk about the "frigging Pantomime," her "ex" and how "glad" she was to be "rid of her," and how "all the gay bars are best avoided," and she was not easily diverted.

She, having just left her partner along with all "her pantomime rubbish," had months of bottled-up emotion, and three pints down, Lesley was simmering with sarcasm as she launched into her descriptive criticism of the Riding Room, a three-point-nine-star gay bar.

Helmut interrupted her. "I am not gay," he muttered.

"That, my friend, is obvious," said Lesley with a tilt of her pint.

Helmut, unsure how to take such a comment, ordered another beer.

After their fourth pint, Lesley and Helmut moved to a table, where his legs sprawled out in front him tripping up the odd drunk.

Lesley pulled out the Stand leaflet poking from Helmut's top pocket and after a quick flick said, "That's your problem."

"Begging your pardon?" said Helmut.

"Tuesday is Red Raw night, or as they laughingly put it here, 'a night of new talent yet to be discovered.'" She drained her pint. "Heard that before." She tossed the leaflet across the bar. "The clue is in the 'raw' so-called talent."

Helmut, with a downcast look, folded up his leaflet. "It is all, as you say, becoming clear," he muttered.

"That's what they said at the panto players," said Lesley, "'make way for new talent.' Sent my ex loopy trying to beat the new talent. And for what? To prance about a stage in thigh-high boots?"

"I have given up on the comedy," he said, trying not to think too much of thigh-high boots.

"You should have tried Friday," said Lesley.

"Maybe skip the clubs," muttered Helmut.

"Mind you still a hit-or-miss," said Lesley.

"I am really more interested in healing than stage," he said.

"Should visit Lochgilphead then, that place could do with some therapy," said Lesley.

Helmut, a literal man, looked up Lochgilphead on his mobile. "And how do you spell this Loch-what?"

Lesley laughed, bemused. "I was joking."

Helmut, engrossed in his mobile Guide to Bonny Scotland app, didn't hear.

"I mean it's hardly worth the two hour drive"—she looked at his app—"or the bus trip."

"Past Loch Lomond," Helmut muttered.

"On a bus?" she said. "Not exactly sightseeing."

He looked up. "Will there be bagpipes?"

"Bagpipes?" laughed Lesley. "On Loch Lomond? What do you think they are, wild animals?"

Helmut, thanks to a few pints, was now in sync with Lesley's barbed comments. He threw his head back and let out a hyena-like laugh that stopped the pub.

"Jesus," muttered Lesley.

Helmut loved to laugh, especially at things no one else saw funny. A date for Helmut usually ended at the first joke.

He stared down at his app. "I come from a small village. It too is full of funny people."

Lesley eyed him suspiciously and sipped her pint. "There is Deirdre's creams, I suppose." She looked at Helmut.

"Creams?"

"Yes, she sells them in her Vegan is the New Black shop."

"Black? Vegan?"

"And Daisy's salon."

"Daisy? Is this not a flower?"

"She does a spot of massage, although I hate to say not on a par with Deirdre's." Lesley wiped her mouth.

"Then why say this?" said Helmut.

Lesley pushed her empty glass towards Helmut. "Funny man, aren't you?"

"You, Lesley, are the first to say this—where I come from, they say *seltsam*."

"What's that mean?"

"Weird."

***

Book 3 ***Panto Girl*** is out now at your favourite store.

I hope you enjoyed Deirdre's adventures inspired by my time performing in the local pantomime although there was no pole dancer. I did once have a go at pole dancing, or rather that sort of dancing without the pole. There were tassels and a video; but that's another story.

You can find me and my groovy blogs at
www.kerrienoor.com
Like me at

facebook.com/kerrienoorwriter
x.com/kezzamac
instagram.com/kerrienoor

THANKYOU'S

Editor– the lovely Sarah Kolb-Williams
Book cover designer–The wonderful libzyyy @ 99 designs
And...
Ye ole Adrishaig Amateur Dramatic Society
We had a lot of fun